HARRY HATES HAIRCUTS

Roxanne Scoville

Illustrated by Dustin Clark

This book is dedicated to all the mothers who are lucky enough to have a Harry in their lives.

Harry H. Pomegranate was an average eight year old boy...

Mostly.

There were some things he *liked* to do like eating candy or throwing his special curve snowball at passing cars.

And there were some things he didn't like, such as taking a bath...

or eating broccoli.

But there was one thing that Harry *really* hated...

Getting a haircut!

Harry always made such a fuss at the barbershop that whenever the barbers saw Harry being dragged up the street by his mother, they would turn out the lights, put the "Out To Lunch" sign up...

...and hide in the back of the room until Harry and his mother were gone.

So Harry's mother started cutting Harry's hair, which was absolute torture for them both.

One day when Harry's hair was looking particularly long, Harry heard his mother calling "Harry! Harry!" in her sweetest voice. Harry knew that this meant...
a haircut!

Harry quietly slipped around the corner of the house hoping to avoid her but she grabbed him and plopped him into a conveniently placed chair right where she found him!

(Who ever said mothers weren't smart?)

Then she whipped out the scissors and began combing through Harry's long hair and suddenly in desperation, Harry jumped out of the chair and screeched, "I hate haircuts! I wish I never had to get a haircut ever again! I hate them--I hate them-- I hate them!!"

Harry's mother lowered her scissors, thought for a moment, and then said "OK" and went into the house. After a moment of shock Harry recovered enough to jump up and run to the park as fast as he could (in case his mother changed her mind).

"Hey, Guys! I don't have to get my hair cut ever again!!"

Harry's buddies couldn't believe it, and one of the smarter boys thought it sounded a little fishy.

A few months later Harry was still really enjoying himself when he started having a problem tripping over things and bumping into people because he couldn't see.

When he couldn't see his schoolwork his grades dropped and Miss Crumple told him that he would have to improve his grades or stay back one grade.

Then one Saturday at baseball practice Harry couldn't see the ball. He couldn't catch either. He couldn't hit the ball. Whenever he threw the ball to someone, it went in the wrong direction.

Harry's friends told him that he had better do something about his hair or he wouldn't be able to play on their team anymore.

But nobody would cut Harry's hair. No matter how hard he pleaded, the barbers still banned him from the barbershop.

Harry's mom said that Harry should stick to his decision not to get a haircut.

So the weeks and months passed by and Harry's hair grew longer...

and longer...

and longer...

and LONGER!

One day, while grocery shopping with his mother, a sweet old lady came up to Harry, patted him softly on the head, and said, "What a darling little girl--and such lovely long hair!"

"That's it!!" Harry yelled. And he yelled so loudly that it startled the little old lady and she fainted into a crate of oranges!

"If you cut my hair" said Harry, "I promise to never complain again. I'll eat my broccoli and even (yuck) take a bath. I'll... I'll even clean my room! So please, PLEASE cut my hair!" Harry pleaded.

Harry's mother smiled a sly smile and took Harry home where she gave him a real SHORT haircut.

Suddenly Harry noticed something wonderful. His head felt deliciously light and cool, and he could actually see where he was going.

At school Miss Crumple didn't recognize Harry. She even called his mother to make sure it was him. And there was an astonishing improvement in Harry's studies because he could finally see the blackboard.

Roxanne Scoville wrote this story in college and then completely forgot about it. Her husband, Craig, discovered the story and tried to keep it a secret as he pursued getting this book published. However, he had to divulge the secret because he needed her input. Despite her best efforts to sabotage the project, this book is dedicated to all of Roxanne's beautiful and wonderful children and grandchildren.

Made in the USA
San Bernardino, CA
29 April 2019